For Barnaby and Tina – M B

This edition published by Scholastic Inc., 557 Broadway, New York,
NY 10012, by arrangement with Little Tiger Press.
SCHOLASTIC and associated logos are trademarks
and/or registered trademarks of Scholastic Inc.
Distributed in Canada by Scholastic Canada Ltd., Markham, Ontario

Original edition published in English by LITTLE TIGER PRESS,
an imprint of Magi Publications, London, England, 2010

Text and illustrations copyright © Matt Buckingham 2010

ISBN: 978-1-84895-073-3

Printed in China

2 4 6 8 10 9 7 5 3 1

Bright Stanley
and the Cave Monster

Matt Buckingham

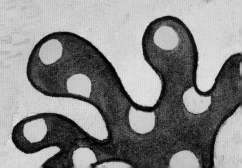

Deep, deep at the bottom of the sea
lived a sparkly little fish called Stanley.
Stanley loved to explore. It was his
favorite thing in the whole, wide world.

One day, as he swam happily along,
Stanley spotted his friends, Percy,
Turtle, and Pufferfish. "Coo-ee!"
he called. "It's me-ee!"

"What's going on?" said Stanley, swimming over.

"We're going to explore this cave!" said Pufferfish, bursting with excitement.

"I'm going in first!" said Turtle.
"No, I am. I'm the bravest!"
said Percy, puffing out his chest.
"Oh, I love adventures!" said
Stanley. "Come on, let's go!"

Inside the cave, there were odd-looking plants and a lot of strange, shadowy shapes.

"What a mysterious place!" exclaimed Stanley.

"It's not scary at all!" boasted Percy,
swimming ahead. "See!"
But just then, he turned and saw . . .

...a **HUGE,** scary monster head

creeping up the wall toward him!

"Hopping herrings!" shrieked Percy.
"It's a sea dragon ready to
gobble us up!"

As quick as a flash, Percy dived behind a big rock, shivering and shaking.

"Oh, Percy," giggled Pufferfish, "you're afraid of shadows!"

"Anyway," boasted Turtle, "we're not afraid of a silly sea dragon!"

"Don't worry, Percy," said Stanley.
"There's nothing to be scared of.
Just stick with me, you'll see!"

The four little friends swam on one by one. The cave was much darker now, and everything seemed strangely quiet.

Out in front, Turtle and Pufferfish began to sing:
  "Oh dragon, oh dragon, if you're there,
  Come out of the dark, if you dare!"
But just then, right in front of them they saw . . .

. . . a
GIGANTIC,
wiggly
tentacle!

PUFF!

"It's a giant squid monster come to squish us!" squeaked Pufferfish, puffing up into a big ball.

"Leaping lobsters!" cried Turtle,
as he quickly hid in his shell.

POP!

"Don't worry!" said Stanley. "There's nothing
to be scared of. They're only shadows!"
"But Stanley," Turtle said timidly,
"I think there really is a monster in here!"

Stanley smiled at his friends. "No, there isn't! Anyway, we can't stop now—we're on an adventure!"

Stanley bravely led the way.
"Coo-ee! It's me-ee, Stan-ley!"
he called with a smile. "We've come
to play, Mr. Squid Sea Dragon!"
Then, from deep within the cave,
came a whispery reply!

"Jumping jellyfish!" cried Stanley.
"The monster is coming!" shrieked Percy,
Turtle, and Pufferfish.

PUFF!

WHOOSH!

POP!

The strange shadows got
closer and closer. Then suddenly,
in a whoosh of bubbles, out popped . . .

. . . . a lot of smiling, shimmering seahorses.
"You're not monsters!" giggled Turtle.
"We were afraid of your shadows!"
laughed Percy.
"Come on," smiled Stanley, "Let's all play!"

And as the new friends played
among the sparkly bubbles,
they all agreed—this had been
the best adventure ever!